Ch...

The flinty glint in ...yan's narrowed dark eyes and her creased forehead threatened a fiery eruption, as she looked up from the picture on the table and then at her mother and then back at the picture. She pushed her glasses up on to her head, and glared fiercely at her mother.

"Mama, do you seriously, actually - I mean - literally, expect me to wear a *lime green* dress with *purple frills?*" she finally hissed.

"Lime Green? It's a...a... monstrosity of a dress. Never! I'd rather wear a bin liner than put on that hideous and ridiculous outfit.

I'll be, literally, a laughing stock. My picture will be pasted all over Snapchat, Facebook, Instagram, whatever. I'll be a meme for all eternity on cyber space."

She took a deep breath and continued her rant.

"And, when I get to be Prime Minister, my enemies will use it to humiliate and destroy me! No way, it's never going to happen; ever!" and giving her mother a look that was a lethal mixture of disgust and defiance across the breakfast table, she threw herself back in her chair, almost, but not quite, toppling backwards.

Her mother held Inaayah's furious gaze calmly and sipped her tea,

"Inaayah dear, the other three maids of honour will be dressed in exactly the same style; I'm sure you will look perfectly lovely.

You know my cousin Kanza is a very creative person. She's sketched the design out with a lot of thought, and I must say it looks, er... very original. This is going to be her big day, her wedding day, and she so wants you to be the chief maid of honour."

Her cajoling smile was met with a scowl, but she ignored it and began to remove the enormous boxes of cereal that seemed to loom over everything on the dining table. Inaayah wasn't going to let her mother off that easily.

"Is that why she's come up with the most horrible combination of lime green and purple?"

she said witheringly, "I seriously doubt how artistic she is. And, I don't care if she wants me to be her 'chief maid of honour', whatever that is. All it means is that I have to stand on the stage with her, literally forever, getting pins and needles in my feet, whilst everyone will stare and laugh at me looking like a... a giant bruised gooseberry and taking pictures of me on their phones."

She snorted loudly in derision, "No thank you, Aunt Kanza! Someone, anyone else is welcome to that honour."

Her younger brother, Sufyaan, was unusually quiet. He chewed his cereal thoughtfully as he listened to his mother and sister. Their father was oblivious to what was going on, his head deep in his laptop, his fingers tapping away furiously. Baby Maariya played happily in her high chair.

"Kanza also wants to have Page boys," continued their mother, as if Inaayah's outburst had never happened, "They'll wear matching outfits with the girls – a green shirt with purple sash and white trousers. Isn't that sweet?"

Sufyaan spluttered, spectacularly scattering half- chewed Cheerios across the table; Maariya laughed and clapped her hands in delight.

"Eeuggh, drat it Sufy! You're disgusting!" shrieked Inaayah, picking bits of Sufyaan's food from her plate with a paper napkin.

"Me? I'm not wearing a sash! Boys don't wear sashes, that's for little girls! And white trousers? That is so not cool!"

"Don't speak with your mouth full," said Mama disapprovingly, "this morning neither of you will go swimming, as the dressmaker is coming in about half an hour to measure you up."

"This is an ambush! How come you never spoke about this wedding before, Mama? You always love talking about these kind of events, like who is doing what and where and all that stuff. Ha! You knew we wouldn't like it, that's why!" Inaayah's voice rose in protest.

"I don't care," said Sufyaan, slurping the last bits of milk from his bowl. "I finished my level ten swimming assessment last week and today I'd only be hanging around waiting for all the others to have their's." He wiped his mouth with the back of his hand, ignoring Inaayah's outraged glare.

For Better or Worse
Written by K.T Ahmed

The flinty glint in Inaayah's narrowed dark eyes and her creased forehead threatened imminent explosions as she looked up from the picture on the table and then at her mother and then back to the picture. "Mama, do you seriously, actually, literally, expect me to wear a lime green dress with purple frills?" her words came out in an astonished h__ |

"But Mama, I don't want to be a page for Aunt Kanza; can't I be the best man? That's what boys do. Maybe the chap she's getting married to doesn't have a brother or someone to be his best man. You need to find out straight away."

"You two are impossible." Mama was rapidly losing her patience, "You should be happy that you've been asked to be part of Kanza's special day. She is very fond of you both, always buying you wonderful birthday presents; taking you out on day trips and being interested in everything you do. Frankly, I'm shocked and upset at your reaction."

"No amount of presents could ever be enough to get me to wear a lime green and purple frilled dress" said Inaayah, taking a vicious bite out of her toast.

"She's taken us to some very boring exhibitions and lots of old houses, full of dead people's stuff; I'm not sure I feel that grateful." added Sufyaan.

His mother glared warningly at him and he quickly looked down into his cereal bowl as if it demanded his utter attention. Inaayah was undaunted.

"Mama, please, you can't want me to wear such a revolting dress?"

she pleaded, pointing to the elaborately hand-painted picture of the dress, which her mother had earlier placed in front of her.

"Just look at it, it's so... so clownish, all puffy and huge; it's so ugly it would be more suited for a Halloween party."

Inaayah's tone became piteous, "And those colours! They don't suit me one little bit! Everyone says I should wear pastels, not loud garish colours. I'll be, literally, mocked by all my cousins and friends. Totally humiliated. Once the pictures go on social media, I'll be a laughing stock; they'll go viral and be there for ever and ever."

She warmed to her theme. "It's definitely against my human rights! In fact, I would say it's almost child abuse. I'm going to be scarred for life by this traumatic experience and all the ridicule I'm going to have to put up with. I'll develop anxiety issues, low self -esteem and end up having to see therapists for the rest of my life and it'll be **all your fault!**"

Actual tears came into her eyes, she brushed them away with the back of her hand.

"'Mental cruelty and harshness', that's the definition of torture," Sufyaan muttered, trying not to catch his mother's eye, "That's what the woman from Childline said, when she came to talk to us about child abuse. It's against the law, all over the world, in fact ..."

"The definition of torture is 'cruel and unusual punishment'" Inaayah corrected him rudely, "that's what the law says; although our legal own expert, Abu, seems totally unaware of the injustices happening right under his nose."

She shot her father a scorching look that had he looked up, he would have gone up in smoke,but he was absorbed in his laptop. He hadn't heard a word of what they had said. Despite it being a Saturday, he was still hard at work preparing for an important case he was going to present at the High Court the following Monday.

Inaayah redirected her ire on her mother.

"I should have been asked, you should've consulted me first. You can't just force people to do things without asking them; it's totally wrong! Totally unfair!"

"And in which planet do parents have to ask their children to be considerate and helpful to their family?" said Mama, icily.

"We are in the twenty first century, aren't we?" continued Inaayah, recklessly. "There is this thing called democracy, isn't there? Where people have individual freedom, to do what they want and not to be forced to do things against their will, right? Everyone has heard of democracy haven't they? It's a basic human right, am I right? And…"

"Thank you for the lecture, Inaayah. I'm glad to know that school isn't wasted on you. Now wrap your extremely clever brain around the fact that, in this house, we are in a timeless zone and all rights are suspended; think of it as a time warp."

Inaayah opened her mouth to speak but was silenced by her mother's upraised finger.

"This matter is not up for negotiation. I don't want to hear another word from either of you. And don't glower at me like that, Inaayah, you don't scare me one iota."

Her mother stood up from the table, "I've already agreed to both of you being part of Kanza's entourage and I will not go back on my promise.

And, Inaayah, at thirteen years old, you need to set a better example to your brother by not having a confrontation for every small matter.

Learn to compromise; believe me, it's a skill that will help you."

Inaayah attempted, feebly, to interrupt,

"No more Inaayah; close your mouth before you catch spiders. Now, both of you, hurry up and clear the table. The dressmaker will want to use it for her bits and bobs."

And with that, Mama picked up the gurgling Maariya and carried her into garden to enjoy the warmth of spring sunshine and escape Inaayah's burst of "But- but - Mama, that's not fair!"

Inaayah pushed her plate of half eaten egg and toast away angrily, banging it against her tumbler of juice, so that the contents sloshed on to the table cloth.

"Drat!!" She stared in disgust as the orange liquid spread across the tablecloth; the weekend ahead had suddenly lost all its shiny promise of bicycle rides in the park and fun with her friends Eliza and Eissa.

"Why do we have to go to all these boring weddings?" she fumed to Sufyaan, as they put the plates and cutlery away into the dishwasher. "Every time, we meet the same people and eat the same kind of food; every time, it's over- greasy samosas, leathery meat kebabs- always served with watery mint chutney and rice with diced mixed vegetables-, which-every time- without- fail, has way too many carrots."

10

"And sit around on uncomfortable chairs with fancy covers and listen to boring people making boring speeches. I hate weddings too." Her father said, rising up from the table. He had been listening after all, but he'd apparently developed a skill by which he only heard bits of conversations.

"I don't mind weddings," said Sufyaan, placidly, putting the milk into the fridge, "Especially if there is some place where we can play. To be honest, I quite like kebabs too, as long as they aren't too hot and spicy." Sufyaan seemed to have recovered from his initial annoyance.

Inaayah gave him a stony look; it was obvious that Sufyaan was not to be relied on in her battle against her mother and Aunt Kanza, he was too easily persuaded.

She would have to use all her ingenuity to get out of being made to look like a fool, in front of hundreds of her family and friends.

"If Mama thinks I'm going to give up without a fight, then she is going to be bitterly disappointed" she vowed to herself, "This is war!"

Chapter 2

Mrs Gomez, the dress maker, arrived with rolls of stiff green material and armfuls of wide purple ribbon. She was a plump, jolly woman, with bright red hair, that fanned out like a halo around her bobbing head. She had round red glasses that constantly slipped down her button nose. Dressed in a crimson shirt and trousers, she looked like a giant tomato. Inaayah could tell immediately that she, too, was not going to be a supporter.

"Come, come, stand on chair," ordered Mrs Gomez, "I measure you for dress." She took out a measuring tape, a stubby bit of pencil and a small tatty notebook. Inaayah pretended that she hadn't heard.

"Inaaaaayaaaah," her mother's warning voice came from the back of the room.

"Alright, alright, I'm going." Inaayah whined, her sense of persecution mounting by the second.

"Hmm, so tall for girl, no?" Mrs Gomez commented, as she scribbled down Inaayah's measurements, "like your brother. But, you no grow too much, ok? Veryvery bad for girl. You be like the giant." She chuckled, her body shaking like a water filled balloon.

'Better to be tall than fat,' thought Inaayah cruelly, and immediately felt ashamed of herself. This made her cross and bad tempered at everyone all over again. Obviously, no one cared about her feelings, all they were bothered about was this ridiculous wedding.

When she told Mrs Gomez she hated the colour of the dress, Mrs Gomez peered at her over the top of her thick round glasses.

"Inaayah, you wear the glittery grey pinafore, the orange spotty t-shirt, and the yellow pedal pushers; no way you know what is fashion."

Inaayah gave her a hard, cold stare, the one which normally fazed most adults, but Mrs Gomez was not to be fazed; she stared straight back at Inaayah with what seemed an amused twinkle in her eyes, infuriating Inaayah even further.

"I hate all of them! Drat this stupid wedding." seethed Inaayah, stomping upstairs. She banged her bedroom door shut extra loudly, and threw herself onto her bed.

"Bossy, horrible people! What do they know about the clothes I like? And anyway, I never asked to be a stupid maid in waiting!"

That was the problem with grown- ups, she thought, as well as being dictatorial, they had delusions that they knew what was best for children, when quite honestly, children were perfectly able to make sensible decisions for themselves.

"And," she shouted angrily to the stuffed animals slumped at the bottom of her bed, "I am NOT a CHILD!" The shabby and worn out cat looked at her blankly, it's neck bent to one side in an apologetic and sad pose.

It was as bad as Inaayah feared; over the next few weeks Mrs Gomez wheezed into the dining room, and with Inaayah standing to attention on a chair or stool, would drape the awful static green fabric around her, prodding and poking her into various poses.

All the while, she would talk through a mouth full of pins, about how Inaayah was going to 'veryvery love this dress I stitch for you,' and how marvellous all the maids of honour would look; and how arty and 'veryvery' wonderful Aunt Kanza was; and how the young man who was going to marry her was 'veryvery, very lucky' to get such a talented and beautiful bride. At the end of each fitting, Inaayah was 'veryvery' ready to murder Mrs Gomez, Aunt Kanza, 'the lucky young man' and the all the people who were subjecting her to this prolonged torment.

To her utter disgust, Sufyaan was enthusiastic about the whole thing. He was chatty and friendly with Mrs Gomez, discussing fashion with her and generally an eager participant. Inaayah heard him in astonishment; she knew he liked to dress nicely, always coordinating his shirt or T-shirt with his trousers, always with matching socks and being the smartest nine year old that she knew, but this was a side to Sufyaan she did not know existed.

"Don't you think, Mrs Gomez, it would be better to wear the purple sash as a cumber band around my waist?" she overhead him say, "it's much more grown up and smarter, don't you think?"

"So true, Sufyaan, is beautiful idea. You veryvery sensitive, veryvery creative. But your sister, ay ay!" Mrs Gomez shook her head sadly, as she carefully carried on pinning and cutting up material. Inaayah snorted in derision and left the room.

"Sufyaan veryvery imaginative!" Mrs Gomez declared admiringly to Mama, "Maybe, he like Lagerfeld or Yves Saint Laurent!"

Mama rolled her eyes in horror, "Please, don't put such ideas into his head; he loves dressing up far too much already. What a situation, a daughter who is at war with me and the world, and a son who is obsessed with style."

Inaayah didn't bother to respond to her mother, because it was the truth.

Inaayah grew to loathe the very sight of lime green. She had nightmares about the dress. In her dreams, she was an enormous, fluorescent green balloon with long purple steamers, floating high up in the sky.

Suddenly, someone, (she never saw their face) came with a giant pin and popped her and she burst into a million small pieces, scattering over the sky. The sound of jeering and laughing from an unseen crowd got louder and louder, as all the green and purple bits of her fell into a pool of dirty, dingy water. She would wake up, sweating and shaking with fear.

Even at school, Inaayah was haunted by the upcoming wedding. Her teachers constantly reprimanded her for being distracted in class and inattentive to her work. She slipped from being the top in her class to third position. Zoe, her best friend began to look bored when Inaayah would start on the subject of the wedding.

"Stop making such a big deal of it. If you really don't want to wear it, tell your mum, or just don't go to the wedding."

"You don't know my mum, Zoe, she's fierce when she's decided on something; my life wouldn't be worth living if I refused to be a maid in waiting."

"Well, why don't you pretend to yourself that's it's fine? Maybe, that will help you get through it."

"I don't want to pretend, why should I? Why can't they think about my feelings? It's not fair."

"Fine, then you have to decide Inaayah, if you do it happy or do it unhappy, it's your choice. Honestly, all this stress over a wedding; I'd just not go."

Inaayah fell silent, she knew that Zoe would never understand why she couldn't refuse to go; in her family, commitments and obligations had to be fulfilled, at all costs; like the time when they had to cancel going to the cinema, just because one of her father's old aunts had a fall and they'd all rushed over to see if she was alright, (even though she was a tough old lady). Inaayah was trapped.

She changed from her usual bright, happy and loving self into a moody, irritating and irritable stranger.

"You're over-reacting Inaayah," her father tried to reason with her when, after another heated session with Mrs Gomez, she vowed that she would rather have appendicitis than go through the ordeal of wearing 'that monstrosity.'

"You'll wear it for a few hours, at the most. The only person giving your clothes a second thought will be you. Everyone else will be preoccupied with the food, catching up with their friends and relatives and being more concerned about how they look themselves. Ask Mama, ask anyone, no one notices what other people are wearing."

"Yea, right, of course I believe you, Abu," replied Inaayah, sarcastically, "At your cousin Adam's wedding, I distinctly remember hearing you say, in what you think is a soft whisper but which everyone at the table, if not the room, could definitely hear, 'what on earth has the bride got on?' Everyone at the table snorted into their napkins to stop themselves from laughing out loud!"

Her father coughed nervously, he remembered that wedding only too well.

"That was different, she was the bride, we're supposed to notice what she wears. I mean, she was dressed in this yellow furry, feathery outfit; she looked like an Easter chicken." he coughed again, unsuccessfully, to hide a snigger.

"Ha!" exclaimed Inaayah, triumphantly, "No one is going to forget that dress are they? Or, the maids of honour, done up in bright yellow, looking like a clutch of yellow chicks!"

"Inaayah, I have never met a girl as obsessive in her dislikes, as you. Why can't you focus on the good rather than the bad, you would be so much happier." Abu threw his hands up in mock despair and went back to making notes on his laptop.

Inaayah regarded him bitterly; parents were so insensitive. She would run away and join a circus, if she knew where there was one, or if she was good at acrobatics, which she wasn't; or, if she liked caravans, which she didn't. It seemed to her that it was her unlucky fate to live with uncaring, callous parents and a disloyal brother, and to suffer the humiliations that they were determined to inflict on her, purely to ruin her life.

Inaayah was going to bed when she overheard her parents talking softly to each other as they cleared up in the kitchen,

"I'm at my wits end, Ummar; she's totally unreasonable and obstinate.I know I was never like this as a child. She must take after your family."

Her father laughed, but in an unamused sort of way.
"She'll grow out of it, Rabia, I'm sure. She's not normally so fanatically hostile. It must be a teenage disorder or something. I mean, she doesn't even care that much about her clothes, yesterday, she was wearing jeans with so many rips, it barely held together, and an oversized jumper, that looked as if the moths had been having a feast with it."

"That child is obdurate, totally obdurate."

Inaayah was so infuriated, she stomped up the stairs, extra loudly, just to let them know she'd heard everything. She immediately went to look up 'Obdurate' in the dictionary and was pleased that to see that it meant 'determined and immovable'. She ignored the 'stubborn' bit.

She was determined not to surrender, even though she knew in her heart that she had lost the battle; her parents weren't going to give in to her because in their opinion, she was being silly and immature.

Inaayah was intelligent enough to know when it was wiser to accept the situation, but this time she couldn't; the dress had come to represent for her something more, her self-respect and individuality. She was far more miserable than her parents realised and even she herself dared to admit.

Chapter 3

The wedding day arrived, bright and warm. The sunshine streaming through the blinds of Inaayah's window lit up the offending dress, which hung on the back of her bedroom door. Inaayah saw it as soon as she opened her eyes and groaned; how quickly the days had passed and now it was THE DAY.

"I'm too ill to go." she whimpered, as Mama came bustling into her room to get her up. It was true, she was feeling sick; sick at the thought of the wedding. Her stomach was somersaulting and her mouth felt as if it was stuffed with cotton wool. Her mother expertly whipped the duvet off the bed, in one swift movement.

"You're cruel and heartless Mama. I've probably got a serious disease that no one has ever heard about.

I'll end up in hospital, with all sorts of tubes going in and out of me, but, you don't even care," wailed Inaayah, trying to pull back her duvet. Her mother towered over her, unmoved by her piteous cries.

"Get up Inaayah, now! Stop playing silly games. Aunty Sophia is here to help get you and Sufy ready. I'm leaving now, for the wedding venue, as I need to help with the flowers and other arrangements. I've no time to waste with you as I have to drop Maariya at your grandmother's.

Also, Inaayah, no more complaints, do you hear me? I want to see you in that hall, in that dress, in a better mood; is that clear?" her mother fixed her with a look that made Inaayah's heart sink,

"Yes, Mama." Her voice was so low, it was barely audible. The taste of defeat was bitter.

Ordinarily, Inaayah was very fond of her Aunty Sophia; they looked very much alike, with the same dark laughing eyes, and a mouth ready to burst into a smile, but, that morning Aunty Sophia was less sympathetic to Inaayah's feeling than even her mother. She laughed and shook her head in amusement at Inaayah's protestations. Inaayah resorted to being as bad tempered and surly as possible.

"Inaayah, you will not provoke me today. What a blessedly beautiful day to have a wedding. It's sunny and warm, the sky clear and blue and the birds are singing away. We're all going to attend a happy event of someone we love, in the company of friends and family. What could be nicer than that, eh?" Aunty Sophia, as bright and merry as the sunshine, plaited Inaayah's thick, unruly hair into an elegant French plait.

Inaayah huffed peevishly, "Actually Aunty Sophia, the weather forecast said it was going to rain later in the afternoon. This is England, the weather is totally unreliable and we could have all four seasons in one day." She hoped it would pour down and dampen everyone's unbearably upbeat spirits.

The sun seemed to mock Inaayah by making her lime green dress glow like a neon light, whilst the purple frills, which ran in multiple horizontal tiers around the wide flounced skirt, down the sleeves and across the bodice,   deepened to a horrible mauve colour.

"I look and feel like a privet hedge invaded by purple ivy." Inaayah complained as they walked to the car.

"Nonsense," said Aunty Sophia, "You look like a pretty girl in a green dress, a nice green dress." Luckily for Aunty Sophia, Inaayah missed the hint of a smile that appeared on the corners of her mouth, otherwise it there might have been bitter words exchanged.

Sufyaan looked very handsome in his suit, he admired himself in the hall mirror before walking out to the car. Seeing the French marigolds crowding the borders of the front garden, he snapped off some of the huge heads and presented them to his father, Aunty Sophia and Inaayah.

"Put these in your button holes, like this, see?" he instructed, "'cos, they smell really nice. Did you know marigolds are a sign of the sun? The Egyptians used to give them as presents to their gods."

"It was the Aztecs, genius." sneered Inaayah, "but, seriously, orange coloured marigolds, on a luminous green shirt with a bright purple cumber band? Not very classy, is it?"
Sufyaan didn't hear her mean comment as he was busy trying to fix the Marigold stem into the top button of his shirt, but Aunty Sophia certainly did; she pulled Inaayah to the side and looked sternly into her eyes,

"Enough of this young lady! Wipe that silly, supercilious smirk off your face this instant! You are going to put on a happy smile, even if I have to paint it on you. This is not about you, Inaayah, it's about Kanza. It's her big day, something that she has been hoping for and planning for a long time; and today it is happening, she is getting married."

Inaayah thought for a moment Aunty Sophia was going to explode in rage, her face was so red.

"In life, young lady, we have to do many things that we don't want to do, just to make those we love, happy. So, no more of this petulant childish behaviour. I want to see a cheery expression, even if it hurts you to do it!"

This was so unlike Aunty Sophia, that Inaayah's eyes filled with unexpected tears. The realisation that she had gone too far and that everyone was angry with her, made her feel wretched. She couldn't quite believe how unpleasantly she had and was behaving. What was the matter with her? To allow a ridiculous dress to ruin her life? She took off her glasses and polished them with the hem of her dress, and sat in a miserable silence that lasted all the journey to the hall.

The traffic into central London was chaotic and busy.

Abu frequently burst out with some very rude and uncomplimentary words for the other drivers. Aunty Sophia said,

"Ummar, please remember, 'little pitchers with big ears'. We don't want the children to start repeating what you say."

"Next time someone wants a swanky do at some fancy West End hotel, I'm going to tell them that they'll have to do without my company, thank you very much. Hell is driving into London on a busy weekend." he grumbled to no one in particular.

"It will be Aunty Sophia, I expect," said Sufyaan with a knowing grin. Aunty Sophia smiled mysteriously. Inaayah studiously ignored them, she just didn't understand this obsession with marriage. Surely, there were more important things in life than getting married, like, being the first astronaut to fly to Mars or discovering the cure to hiccups? Why did people think that being tied to another person for the rest of your life was so brilliant? In her class most of her friends' parents were divorced or separated. Her parents were fine, but she guessed that was because they loved each other very much and tried to be considerate and kind to each other, despite Abu working so hard.Most adults were confused and deluded, she reasoned, no wonder the world was in such a terrible situation, what with global warming, the icebergs melting and all the insects becoming extinct.

By the time they arrived at the venue, they were all stiff and tired. Inaayah was still smouldering silently; she noted with grim satisfaction that her dress was creased and some of the frills no longer lay down flat against the dress but pointed upwards, as if they wanted to fly off the dress in disgust.

"Such a stupid dress," she thought, "not only does it look ugly, it's totally impractical."

Her angry misery returned with a vengeance.

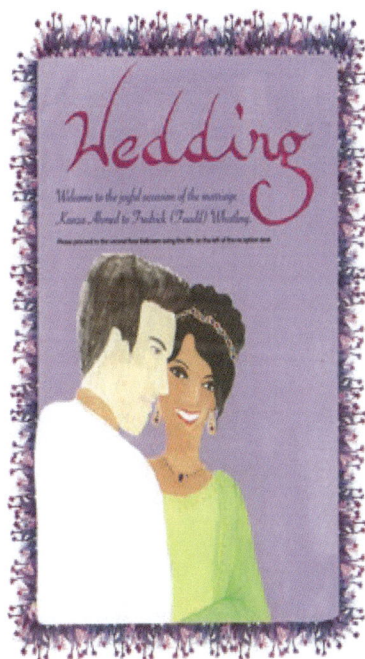

Chapter 4

The children walked into the foyer with Aunty Sophia whilst their father parked the car. At the entrance there was a huge board which read in large letters:

'Welcome to the joyful occasion of the marriage of Kanza Ahmed to Fredrick (Faadil) Whatling.'

Then, in smaller letters,

'Please proceed to the second floor Ballroom using the lifts on the left of the reception desk.'

Below the announcement was a huge colour cameo picture of Kanza looking beautiful; her dark long hair was arranged in artistic coils on the top her head, like a Roman goddess, and covered with small shiny jewels; her dark eyes looked even larger in her pale face, with a beaming smile which lit up her face.

"She's very pretty," observed Sufyaan, "I bet her husband won't be.

I've noticed that about lots of nice looking girls, that they marry men who are quite ugly, but have a lots of money."

"That's very cynical for someone so young," remarked Aunty Sophia, "Women do marry men who aren't rich, if they are kind and good, Sufyaan."

"What's 'cynical'?" asked Sufyaan, staring around the foyer.

"It means that you don't have a very good opinion of people's behaviour, like saying that girls only marry for money." Aunty Sophia replied.

"Everyone pretends they don't," retorted Inaayah, "but whenever you hear someone is about to get married, the first thing I hear from the adults, especially the aunties and grannies, is 'what does he do? How much does he earn? Does he own a house?'"

"I can't disagree with you there, Inaayah, but thankfully, not everyone is like that, people do marry because they love one another and see past looks and money." laughed her Aunty, "but look, here's a picture of Frederick and he doesn't look ugly, does he?"

There was a picture of the groom next to Kanza's. It showed a man with a long face, elongated even more by a thin aquiline nose and sleepy grey eyes. His mouth wore a half smile, as if it had given up midway and made do with a small stretch.

Looking at the pictures, it was impossible to imagine that they had anything in common, let alone that they were about to be married; he was so serious and she so bubbly and full of life. More of the mysteries of 'so called love', thought Inaayah in bafflement.

The lobby of the hotel was a crush of bright colours and heavy perfume. Men, women and children thronged in the corridors and the lobby, waving and shouting out greetings to one another above the persistent beat of Indian songs blaring out of the loudspeakers.

Inaayah recognised many of them as being friends and family members; amongst them she spotted the other maids of honour and the boy pages by the flashes of green and purple.

"They look absolutely horrible," she thought with grim satisfaction, "but, that's no satisfaction to me because it means that I look just as awful."

She felt resentful and miserable again, wishing she could magically disappear and never have to see any of these people ever again.

"It's very noisy!" shouted Sufyaan to Inaayah, his hands over his ears, "I can't even hear myself think!"

Inaayah noticed a magnificant wooden staircase to the side of the lifts. She was intrigued by it's hugeness and the splendour of the wooden balustrade; what fun it would be to se how far up it went and escape the noisy crowd.

"Let's go and explore the stairs," she went closer to Aunty Sophia and Sufyaan, to shout into their ears.

"What?" yelled back Aunty Sophia, clicking her teeth in disappointment, as yet another lift went up and they were left standing at the back of the queue.

Inaayah pointed to her left. Sufyaan's eyes widened in excitement.

"Wow, its a spiral staircase! Look, it goes right up to the roof, like a corkscrew. Wouldn't it be fun to slide down the swirly bannisters, all the way from the very top to the bottom?"

Sufyaan ran towards the stairs as if he would do it immediately.

Aunty Sophia shouted "Don't you dare Sufyaan!" she looked warningly at Inaayah,

"Inaayah, you're the eldest, I expect you to make sure that Sufyaan doesn't do anything silly or dangerous. I don't want you to let me down; you have to set a better example."

"You mean like, bumps down the stairs? Or, abseil down the front of the hotel?" Inaayah joked, and seeing her aunty's horrified expression added quickly,

"Just a joke Aunty Sophia, chill please."
Aunty Sophia beamed,

"Inaayah, that is the first smile I've seen from you today. How much prettier you look when you don't have a constant scowl on your face; do try and keep it that way, please."

This only resulted in the scowl instantly returning to Inaayah's face. Aunty Sophia gave a sigh and waved them off, telling them she would wait for the lifts.

The children raced up the red carpeted stairs. The gilt balustrade curved upwards in graceful sweeps of polished dark wood. When they looked down, it was if they were looking through a telescope the wrong way round; everyone below looked smaller. Even the music became muted, with only the occasional deep beat floating to their ears.

Above them, the stairs twisted and twirled until they seemed to disappear into the sky through the huge glass dome on the top. It was quite magnificent.

"We'd better return to the main hall, Sufy," said Inaayah, when they had puffed their way to the fourth floor, "I don't want to be told off by Aunty Sophia again."

"I don't know why you don't relax and enjoy yourself, Inaayah. You always seem in a bad mood these days. It's very hard being with you because you're no fun anymore."

"Sorry, Sufy, you're right." admitted Inaayah, "I promise to try to not be so miserable. Race you to the second floor!"

Chapter 5

The children returned to the second floor ballroom out of breath and flushed. As they stepped into the ballroom, Inaayah gave an involuntary gasp of admiration, everything looked so very majestic and beautiful.

The enormous room was set out with tables and chairs in white linen and green and purple ribbons. There were about thirty tables, each seating about ten people; and each table had a centrepiece of green and purple flowers. Swags of green and purple material were draped over throne like couch, which was covered in gold and white cloth; presumably, that would be where the bride and groom would be seated, just like royalty.

A low, constant babble of voices filled the air as the guests chatted and mingled, along with the occasional shrieks and laughter of small children running around. A guitarist was playing some pleasant melodies, there was a happy and joyful atmosphere in the room.

Inaayah was about to suggest to Sufyaan that they walk around and explore the room further, when someone prodded her in the back. She smelt her overpowering perfume before she saw her, it was one of Kanza's fashionable friends.

"Hurry up you two," she scolded, in a thin screechy voice, "You're late, all the other children are here. You're the only two not in place."

She pushed them forward with her scarlet tipped fingers. Her high heels clicked importantly, like castanets, on the parquet flooring.

Inaayah decided immediately that she didn't like her. "You don't have to push so hard," she snapped, "We're here now, aren't we?"

"Sorry, sorry, but we are running late." said the young woman, flustered by Inaayah's curt tone, "The ceremony starts in fifteen minutes, when the Imam arrives. All the guests are here and you have to be in position too. We're all waiting for the groom to show up and then off we go with the big event."

The other maids of honour were standing in stiff attention at one side of the side room, with the pages lined up opposite them; all had a self -conscious air that made them awkward and shy. They didn't even look at one another, let alone talk.

Kanza was seated in the middle of the room; Inaayah counted at least six women fussing over her and that was not including a swarm of others, all swirling around, twittering loudly to everyone and no one in particular. They were like a pandemonium of brightly coloured parrots, squabbling over a piece of fruit.

Inaayah stepped closer to take a peek at Kanza. She was dressed in a dress of pale green silk, like the newest and freshest leaf in spring. A neat, purple band encircled her waist and tiny sparkling amethysts and sapphires twinkled in her hair, whilst larger gems dangled luxuriously from her ears and her neck.

Inaayah gazed at her in a mixture of fury and admiration. Kanza looked stunning in her outfit. The shimmering, soft green suited her perfectly and the iridescent purple was used sparingly and to the maximum effect.

"So, why, oh why, did she condemn us to this horrid, fluorescent lime green? She's done it on purpose, to make herself look prettier, that's why," she thought resentfully. "it's the only explanation, has to be. I'm never, ever going to forgive her." She gave a furious toss of her head and joined the girls on their side of the room.

Sufyaan walked nonchalantly up to the boys, ignoring their curious stares, which turned to disapproval, when they noticed his cumber band, so different the purple sashes that they had draped across their bodies.

One of the pages, a little boy of about five years old, with his thumb stuck in his mouth, announced loudly,

"I wanna it like wot yous got."

He pulled at his sash, his tongue stuck out in concentration.

"It's easy, just wrap the sash around the waist, like I've done it, see?" Sufyaan said, in a friendly helpful kind of voice.

"No, you can't, Ayden," snapped an older boy, slapping the little boy's hands down, whilst fixing a frosty glare at Sufyaan, "You're not allowed to mess around with your clothes."

"But I wanna!" insisted the child, his bottom lip quivering dangerously; he pulled the sash down his shoulders, so that it sat gathered around his small protruding tummy.

40

"You are allowed to, no one minds." Sufyaan said kindly, "Mrs Gomez, who made the outfits said it was more, sofistic..., more sofisfit... any way, whatever, she said that having a cumber band- that's what it's called- looked better around the waist than across the chest. It was my idea though."

"Are you trying to make trouble or do you think you're some kind of fashion guru? Don't try to be a smarty-pants, alright?" The big boy moved aggressively towards Sufyaan, who said in a conciliatory tone,

"Don't be so touchy, keep your sash on. I don't care, it's up to you. You can wear your sash how you want, It's a free world. I think I look smart and sofistimated, with a cumber band, but you can do whatever you like."

Sufyaan stepped back and gave the boy a look exactly like Mrs Gomez did when she wanted to judge how well something fitted.

"Fact is, the way you're wearing it, you look like you're in an Irish dancing competition."

Inaayah looked on with alarm, as the big boy's face deepened into a fiery colour; but Sufyaan carried on, oblivious to the boy's fury,

"I went to watch an Irish dancing competition once. It was really interesting, because they dance with their arms dead straight to their sides, but their feet move at, like, a million miles an hour; tickety tick, tickety tick. It gets boring after a while, but my friend, who was dancing, he came third and he got a medal and…"

"Shut it!" screamed the older boy, his face now blotchy with rage. "No one wants to know about your stupid friend, or stupid Irish dancing, or stupid cumber bands!"

Inaayah was over in a flash; she couldn't stand back and see her brother threatened, even though he was perfectly able to defend himself and wouldn't welcome her interference.
"Hey, leave my brother alone!" she wedged herself between the boy and Sufyaan.

"He's your brother is he? Well, you should teach him better manners then; he shouldn't go around showing off about fashion and stupid cumber bands and blabbing on about Irish dancing and other garbage."
"He's only giving you an opinion, you don't have to follow it, he can say what he wants. Anyway, he's right, those sashes do look silly."

Inaayah tossed her head scornfully, adding under her breath, 'we all look silly and ridiculous, if we're honest.'

"I can fight my own battles, Inaayah," said Sufyaan, in an offended tone to Inaayah.

"No, little babykins needs his big sister to stick up for him," mocked the boy.

"Right, now I'll have to fight you." Sufyaan took up a boxing stance, his feet planted apart and his fists bunched at face level, "you've asked for it and I'm going to give it to you, you can't get away with being rude. I better warn you that I am a champion boxer."

"Nobody is fighting anyone!" Inaayah tried not to raise her voice, in case any of the aunties decided to investigate what was going on.

"He started it!" said Sufyaan pointing at the boy.

"No, you did, twit face!" spat the other boy.

By this time the other maids of honour had joined them. One girl, about Inaayah's age, asked disagreeably,

"What are you fighting about? Not really very appropriate, is it, to scrap at a wedding?" She turned to the older boy, "Zack, Mum will give you a hiding if you get into any more fights."

Zack gave his sister a look full of loathing.

"Oh, of course, Mona, whatever you say. Miss bossy boots!" and he stalked off to the other end of the room.

The girl turned to Inaayah, "Your brother should keep his mouth shut." she said sharply.

Before Inaayah could open her mouth to reply to this new insult, the smallest maid of honour, who had been busy picking her nose up to this point, looked up at Inaayah and said sweetly,

"you looketh like a giant goothberry."

The child had the face of an angel, with big, innocent brown eyes and a small rosebud mouth. Her long tawny hair was tied in two bunches on either side of her head with purple ribbon and she spoke with a slight lisp. she was obvioulsy the twin to the little boy.

"That's not kind, Zahra," said Mona. "you shouldn't go around saying things like that to people you don't know." But she sniggered loudly.

"She doeth too, like a fat gween caterpillar- with purple thpikes- thath's eaten a cow," replied the little girl more firmly.

Inaayah gave the child a look of contempt,

"Well, you aren't much better; if I'm a giant caterpillar, you're a smaller one then."

"No, I'm not," Zahra looked quite unmoved by Inaayah's retort, "You're a big, gween rathberry lolly, all melty and thicky."

"Listen, you little shrimp," said Inaayah, through gritted teeth, "stop being annoying; just because you're small doesn't mean you can go around being rude to people."

"Not wude," said the child defiantly. "And, your dreth is puffy and ugly, like a gweat big gween frog!"

"Well, if you want to swap insults, then I say you look like a blob of sticky, slobbery, slimy snot!" snapped Inaayah, outraged by the child's cheekiness.

"I'm not thnot!" wailed the child, her face crumbling in distress, "thnot is dirty and horrible!"

"Why did you have to say such a mean and disgusting thing to my sister?" demanded Mona, "you've made her cry, you big bully!" and she gave Inaayah a violent shove.

45

Inaayah shoved her back, the girl gave her another push and Inaayah shoved back again, harder. The other girls started to chant, "fight, fight, fight!"

The women looked around in alarm to see Inaayah and Mona trading pushes and behaving in the most unladylike manner.

"Girls, girls," said the young woman who had brought Inaayah and Sufyaan upstairs in a quavery voice, "No fighting please. We're stressed enough already. Dear Kanza is beside herself because Frederick isn't here yet, and no one can contact him. If she hears the maids of honour bickering like cats, she'll be even more distressed."

Inaayah and Mona both looked down at their feet, Inaayah was mortified. Mona muttered,

"Sorry, Aunt Neena, it won't happen again." But as soon as Aunt Neena was out of earshot, she mouthed menacingly at Inaayah, "I'm not finished with you yet; I know who you are, Inaayah."

Inaayah shot back, hotly, "I'll be ready for you."

But, she was shaken by the look of animosity which the other three maids of honour gave her. What was happening? Everyone was against her. She loathed everyone and everything; she wanted the ground to open and swallow her, anything to get away from these horrible children and this awful situation.

Chapter 6

Inaayah slipped out of the side room and into the main hall. Sufyaan, who had watched Inaayah's altercation with the older girl with trepidation, ran after her.

"I hate weddings! I'm never going to get married and you mustn't either Sufyaan!" cried Inaayah,upset almost to the point of tears,

"All this fuss, for what? Just so that they can tell all the world that they're going to live together. Who cares anyway? They should go and get married on a desert island or the Arctic Circle, or even the moon! Instead, they expect everyone to get dressed like clowns and hang around boring ball rooms. What a complete waste of time!" Her cheeks burned with anger.

"People mostly like weddings," said Sufyaan affably, he slipped his arm into Inaayah's, and she appreciated his kind gesture. He cleverly changed the subject.

"I'm hungry Inaayah, it's ages since we had breakfast; perhaps that's why you're being 'h'angry', like Mama says."

At the mention of food, Inaayah's stomach rumbled with hunger and she forgot about being disagreeable. Perhaps all her bad temper was due to not having had breakfast that morning and now it was almost two o'clock in the afternoon.

"I think you're right, Sufyaan, I am starving, too." she replied, "Let's go and see what's on offer in the main room."

They peeked into the ballroom; all the tables were now fully occupied and there was an expectant air in the room; people were straining to see if they could spot the bride or groom. The guitarist had gone and piped music could be heard, the voice of a man singing a slow, mournful song, which Inaayah thought was most unsuitable for a wedding. What a strange wedding this was turning out to be.

After inspecting the nuts and fruit piled high on every table, the children agreed that they wasn't what they wanted.

As they were going out, Inaayah noticed an elderly couple, talking earnestly together in a corner near to the door. The lady was dressed in a powder blue skirt and jacket and on her head she wore a hat with enormously long ostrich feathers which threatened to poke anyone unlucky to come within meter of them in the eye.

The man was tall and dressed in a smart suit with tails and a top hat. However, it wasn't their clothes that made Inaayah pay careful attention to them, the wedding guests were dressed in every sort of outfit, from suits to saris to sarongs, but the fact that they were looking towards the door anxiously and the lady was dabbing at her eyes as if she was crying and the man was patting her arm gently, as if to console her.

'I wonder who they are and why they're so upset?' she thought, 'they definitely aren't very happy.' But, before she could puzzle over them any further, she felt herself being pulled out of the room into the corridor by Suyfyaan.

He steered her into a small room off the hall from where the most delicious savoury smells were wafting out.Inaayah felt her stomach rumble again.

Gathered outside the room were the silver service staff, the waiters and waitresses, shuffling restlessly, waiting for instructions to start serving the food.

One of the waiters was amusing himself by making shapes out of the paper napkins, he looked the friendliest of them so Inaayah walked over to him.

"That's clever," she said admiringly, pointing to a swan that had been magically created by folding the napkin. "what else can you make?"

"Lots of things" replied the young man, handing the napkin to Sufyaan, with a smile. "When I was a steward on a cruise ship, I had to learn how to shape elephants, swans, even monkeys from the towels in the passengers's rooms. It's called origami."

"Wow," Sufyaan inspected his swan admiringly, "That's so cool. Could you show me some more?"

"Nope, cannot do, not possible; no, no, no. I have to be ready to serve the food, and if the Chief catches me messing around, I could be sacked."

"We wouldn't want you to be sacked, honestly," Inaayah said in her politest voice, "But do you have any snacks we could have please? We're really hungry."
"I get it, you're trying to butter me up so you can sneak some food, eh?"
Sufyaan grinned broadly, "No, honestly, we're really impressed with your animals aren't we, Inaayah?"

"Yes, we are, I would love to learn to do what you're doing. But we do want something; if there is any food you can get us, we'll be so, so, grateful because we haven't eaten for hours and hours, and we're literally starving."

"Plus, we'll be your friends for ever and ever!" finished Sufyaan earnestly.

The young waiter laughed loudly and disappeared into the room behind him.

"Here," he said, when he returned. He passed them a bulging white napkin. "Now leg it, before the boss comes. Oh, I'm Jayson by the way." He gave the children a conspiratorial wink.

"Thanks, Jayson," said Inaayah, "I'm Inaayah and this is Sufyaan, my brother. This is so kind of you, we shan't forget it. Bye, we'll see you in a bit."

Inaayah hurried Sufyaan away as a hard faced man, in a badly fitting suit, bore down on the waiters; she was anxious not to cross him, just in case he was the 'chief' that Jayson was worried about.

"Jayson was nice wasn't he" said Sufyaan, through a mouthful of hot chicken samosa, as they walked away from the hall.

"Yes, he was," agreed Inaayah, she felt a lot better now that she had some food inside her.

"I want to see what's up there, at the top of these stairs, Sufyaan. I saw a sign saying something about a roof garden; the views must be fantastic, we could probably see all the way to Watford, I'm sure."

Sufyaan nodded in agreement, his mouth was too full to speak, but he gave a happy smile to show that he was pleased that Inaayah was back to her usual fun self.

They climbed up at least three or four floors before finally arriving at the door which opened onto the roof; but it didn't look like any ordinary door that guests might use, more like a security door as it was made of heavy metal and had a bar across it with the words: 'Alarmed door, no unauthorised person allowed',
written in large yellow letters.
"It's unlocked," observed Inaayah, pushing it open a little more, "looks like somebody's already up here."

A small voice in her head told her that it wasn't a good idea to go out, but she ignored it, anything was better than returning to the wedding party.

"Perhaps, we should go back downstairs, Inaayah" suggested Sufyaan nervously; he didn't want to get into trouble, or be late for the wedding.

"We'll only be here for a minute," said Inaayah stepping out on to the rooftop, "It would be a shame not to see the views from here." She took a deep breath; the coolness was welcome after the stale, hot air of the ballroom.

Chapter 7

A sharp gust of wind whipped around them, so that Inaayah couldn't say whether it was that, or the wonderful panorama of London spread out before her that made her catch her breath. The landmarks of London- the Houses of Parliament, the London Eye, and the magnificent St Paul's Cathedral, the latter dwarfed between the forest of monstrous high rise glass offices, were arranged before them.

The River Thames shimmered and snaked in the distance like a silver chain whilst the ships and boats bobbed along merrily. Beyond, the green spaces of Hampstead Heath lay spread out, like a tablecloth.

"Wow!" Inaayah and Sufyaan breathed out, at the same time. The vista before them was awe inspiring. Inaayah excitedly pointed out Somerset House where they had gone ice skating the previous winter.

They were so engrossed in the views that when there was a loud 'Bang' behind them, they were taken by surprise.

"What was that?" Sufyaan spun around, "it sounded like a door slamming shut."

"It's the door we came through," replied Inaayah, "the wind must have caused it to shut." She looked at Sufyaan uneasily, as it dawned on her that the door could only be opened from inside the building.

"Drat and double drat!" Inaayah ran to the door and pushed at it, desperately hoping it would open, but it would not budge. 'Now we're in trouble' she thought, 'I wish I'd listened to that voice telling me not to come here.'

"There must be a handle somewhere," Sufyaan examined the door carefully. Inaayah prayed that they would spot a little catch or lever that would open the door. There was none.

"Oh, Goodness! We're stuck here on the roof!" she cried in dismay, "No one knows where we are and even if they look for us they won't find us!"

Her heart raced with panic; Mama's and Aunty Sophia's words repeated themselves in her mind. She was going to be in deep trouble now.

"I'll shout, everyone says I have a loud voice" said Sufyaan. He put his mouth close to the door and called out at the top of his voice,

"Help! Open the door, we're stuck on the top of the hotel! Help!"

Inaayah joined him, "Help! Help! Open the door!"

They banged at the door furiously, but it was obvious that their cries could not reach the ears of anyone below.

Inaayah ran to the edge of the roof where a narrow, low wall acted as the only barrier between the roof top and the pavement below. She leaned over, down below the tops of people's heads looked like marbles rolling around, whilst the cars looked like toys on a paper track. Sufyaan joined her; together they began to shout as loudly as they could,

"Help! Somebody, anybody! Look up, Oh please! We're here, up on the roof!"

"We're stuck on the rooftop! Help! Help!"

"No one can hear you," a sad and gentle voice spoke behind them; the children almost lost their grip on the wall with shock. They scrambled quickly to their feet.

59

The man standing in front of them was tall and thin. He wore a long, cream and gold brocade tunic, matching pants, and fancy gold slippers that curled up on the toes, like a lizard's tongue. His wispy blonde hair was tousled and windswept, and his long face and nose gave him the look of a mournful bloodhound.

"The wind carries away your voice." He waved a long elegant hand in the air, whether to catch the words or wave them on, it was hard to tell. "It blows harder and colder up here." He shivered and the children suddenly realised that they too, were chilly.

Inaayah studied him intently, she was sure she had seen that face before, the slightly elongated chin and those deep set grey eyes seemed very familiar.

"You're Mr Fredrick Whatling! The bridegroom!" she exclaimed finally, "Everyone is looking for you down in the hall. What are you doing here?"

The man's face assumed an even more gloomy expression.

"Are they?"He didn't seem to care, "Well, here I am. No one's come looking for me, so I don't suppose it's such a big deal."

Inaayah and Sufyaan exchanged astonished looks, the man was clearly not right in his head.

"Er, actually it is a very big deal," said Inaayah carefully, just in case he was actually a little crazy, "without you the wedding can't go ahead." She couldn't believe the man was running away from his own wedding.

Sufyaan was less diplomatic, "You're holding up the whole show. If you had been downstairs, where you should have been, then we wouldn't have got into a fight with the other kids and we wouldn't be up here.

In fact, because of you, all the guests are starving, the waiters are hanging around with nothing to do; and I bet they won't get paid extra when they have to work for longer. And all because you couldn't be bothered to be on time at your own wedding, Huh, some people!" He scowled and crossed his arms fiercely. Inaayah gave him a sharp nudge with her elbow, she didn't know what had come over Sufyaan, he was usually so good natured.

Sufyaan said furiously, "What did you do that for, Inaayah? It's true, I didn't say anything wrong! He is holding everything up, that Aunty Neena said so!" and he went off in a huff, to sit down with his back to the door that lead back to food and warmth, if only it would open.

Fredrick Whatling, horror struck, turned first towards Sufyaan and then Inaayah.

"I didn't realise I've been up so long," he finally stammered, "I don't have my phone on me or anything because these ridiculous clothes don't have any pockets at all. It was only when I got up here that I realised that I'd left it downstairs, in my rucksack." He rubbed the side of his head, as if he had a headache.

"To be honest, I was actually pleased at first, because I wanted some quiet time to think and clear my head." His whole body seemed to slump in misery.

A sudden flurry of air whipped Inaayah's dress into a whirl of green and purple.

"Drat this stupid dress! How I hate it!" she tried to pull it down but the wind seemed just as determined to give it a life of its own. In frustration, she sat down next to Sufyaan, tucking every possible inch of it under her.
Everything that could go wrong, was going wrong!

Chapter 8

Inaayah looked up at the gangly figure of the groom who was now nervously biting his under lip and cracking his knuckles in a loud and excruciating manner. She felt both sorry and irritated at him. Like Sufyaan, she decided that all of this was his fault, but she could also see that he seemed to suffering from an agony of feelings.

Even though he was a grown man and should be the master of his own life, he'd no choice but to dress up like a character out of Disney's Aladdin. She too, had been forced against her will to put on this horrible mess of a dress, which despite all the metres and metres of material that had been used, was still not substantial enough to keep out the wind. Now, all three of them were stuck on the rooftop, without anyone knowing their whereabouts. Her throat felt tight with anxiety.

"Please don't do that," she snapped, as Frederick continued to crack his knuckles. "It's terribly bad for you; My Nana says it causes arthritis when you get older."

"I suppose as you're old anyway, it doesn't matter," added Sufyaan callously, "You don't have much hair, and from the way it's blowing around, you soon won't have any left at all."

Inaayah elbowed him again, "Shush Sufy, you're being unkind and not very helpful." She gave Fredrick a smile. "He doesn't really mean it; he's overtired and we've just had a stupid fight with the other children downstairs. That's why we came up here, just like you to get away from everyone."

She was surprised at herself for telling this stranger so much, but it was if she had known him for a long time and understood his situation, it was so much like hers.

"Why don't you sit down? The wind doesn't seem to catch you here as much." She shuffled to make space for him, causing Sufyaan to complain,

"Watch it Inaayah! you nearly shoved me off the doorstep."

Fredrick sat down next to them, he had stopped cracking his knuckles and was lacing and unlacing his fingers as if he was knitting with them, his face a picture of misery.

"Oh God, I've made such a mess of things!" he sounded ready to cry, "I mean, I do love Kanza, I really do but it's been all too much. First, the becoming a Muslim, which is fine, I mean, I am happy about that, it was a small step from being a Christian to a Muslim; but then having to deal with her enormous family, that's been hard.

On top of that, I have to pretend that I like this huge, extravagant hoo-ha of a wedding, with hundreds of people, in a flashy place like this, it's too much." He flung out his long arms suddenly, so that he nearly hit Inaayah and Sufyaan.

"You've become a Muslim?" Sufyaan was impressed, "seriously? that's cool! Were you forced into it or did you want to do it?"

"No, I wasn't forced, I spent a year studying beforehand. Kanza chose my Muslim name, Faadil and I'm happy with it, but it's all very surreal. My parents have been very supportive. They're very fond of Kanza and her family, but for me it's been a bit overwhelming."

"I think I saw them, your parents, I mean," said Inaayah, "They were looking very upset, especially your mum. She's the one wearing the enormous hat, isn't she?"

"What? When? How do you know?"

"I saw them both, your mum and your dad, downstairs. I would say they're pretty worried about what's happened to you."

"Oh Lord, what a mess I've made of things! Poor mum, she always gets nervous before big events, she's probably feeling sick!"

"I bet she's more than sick now," muttered Sufyaan, quite heartlessly, in Inaayah's opinion.

"Well, I didn't mean to upset anyone. I just came up here to sort my thoughts out, you know what I mean?"

Inaayah certainly did understand, it was unbearable to be put into situations were you felt you had no choice. Frederick cracked his knuckles more furiously.

Frederick gave a nervous laugh, "Listen to me, trying to explain myself to children; as if you could possibly understand. Ignore me, you two; let's just figure a way to get off from this rooftop, otherwise we might find ourselves spending the night here."

"Excuse me," said Inaayah, her dignity stung, "we're not children! I'm thirteen and Sufyaan is ten. I'm sick of people treating me like a child! In some parts of the world, I would be out working and supporting my family."

"Yes," nodded Sufyaan, "In Asia, they use child labour to make bricks, which is really cruel, we don't have to do that, but we're still practically grown up, though not old grown up, like you, but grown up enough to be able to look after ourselves."

"My sincere apologies." said Fredrick apologetically. Inaayah thought she detected his eyes twinkle with amusement, but she didn't mind because he had been so horribly sad before and she was feeling a bit more forgiving.

"Apology accepted," she said graciously, "It must be difficult for you to have to change so much about yourself, just so that you can marry Kanza."

"You're probably thinking, 'is she worth it?'" butted in Sufyaan, "I have to say that she is a bit weird. I mean the way she likes spending all her time in old houses and going on and on about rocks and stones. You have to admit that's loopy, but when you marry someone I suppose you have to accept their crazy bad bits as well as the nice bits; that's why they say 'for better or worse' when people get married in all the films."

67

"Luckily Kanza hasn't too many 'worse bits' as you put it." Fredrick smiled, "It's nice to know that Kanza likes to look at rocks, even when she's not with me, because I'm a geologist and I study rocks all the time; it's my job. I specialise in the study of rocks or Petrology."

"Wow," said Inaayah, "we're doing geography at school and we looked at some rocks and it turned out they weren't rocks at all, but fossilized elephant poo, called coprolite. There were even the imprints of bits of fern inside, so we could tell what the elephant had eaten."

"That's gross!" said Sufyaan, his eyes shining with delight, "I want to see some copro... whatever it's called, too,"
"Coprolite, Sufyaan, COPROLITE." Inaayah said in a superior tone. Sufyaan ignored her.

"I have a huge coprolite at home." Fredrick made a large circle with both his hands, "We think it belonged to a Sabre Tooth Tiger or some other predator mammal, because there are small bones visible, probably those of a gerbil like creature that it had eaten."

"That's a massive poop! The size of a football! Can we come and see it?" demanded Sufyaan, "Now that you're part of the family, we'll be able visit each other all the time."

He seemed to have forgotten his early animosity towards him. Inaayah gave him another shove with her elbow for being so pushy. Sometimes, she felt Sufy forgot his manners too easily.

At Sufyaan's reminder, Fredrick's face fell into gloom again. "I'm not sure what's going to happen at this moment. I've let Kanza down by hiding myself away here, whilst she's worried sick downstairs. I should be with her." He looked sadly up to the sky, as if asking for divine intervention, but the grey clouds only promised rain.

Chapter 9

Inaayah decided that this was a situation where she had to step up and be the adult. Her mother had told her many times that being mature was not about how old you were or how big, but about being sensible and doing the right thing, at the right time. This was one of those times, the future happiness of Aunt Kanza depended on her and she couldn't let her down, despite how she had tried to ruin her life with the hideous maid of honour dress.

"You have to go downstairs and marry her, like you promised. After all you love her don't you?" she copied her mother's voice when she was being 'firm and reasonable'.

Fredrick nodded; he was cracking his knuckles again, but Inaayah ignored it since she had more serious matters to deal with first.

"Well, then? Just because you have to do something which is new and scary for you, something which you're not comfortable about doing, it's not a reason to let down someone who is depending on you, not just at this moment, but for the rest of their life."

" She stopped, unsure if she had gone too far, but Fredrick was listening, his head turned strangely upwards, as if he was receiving advice from above.

"Sometimes," continued Inaayah boldly, "we have to do things we don't like for the people we love, especially if those things are not really that important, but feel important to the other person; I mean, like wearing stupid clothes or sitting through a boring wedding. After all, it's just for a few hours isn't it? It's soon over and we can get back to what we really want to do." She looked encouragingly at Frederick.

Sufyaan clapped his hands, "Bravo, Inaayah! I'm glad that you're not upset anymore about your dress; although I have to be honest, it's a very ugly dress."

Inaayah turned on him, "You little liar! You told me it looked fine! I'll never believe you again! Ever! Don't think I am going to forget this, Sufyaan!" She quickly regained her composure and turned to Fredrick,

" First of all, I think we need to get down from here and get you married, without wasting any more time, don't you? So, do you have a plan?"

Fredrick seemed to be lost in thought, so Inaayah repeated her question, this time accompanied by a friendly little kick to his foot; she was getting cold out on the roof now that the sun had disappeared behind thick grey clouds and the wind was sharper. She was right about the weather becoming rainy, but it seemed that she would be the one who would be rained on, not the others who were safely indoors. She supposed it served her right for being such a grump.

"I don't know," Fredrick got up and spread out his hands, "I don't have a phone, like I told you, this outfit doesn't have a single pocket, not even for a tissue to wipe my nose." He sniffed dramatically, the cold wind was making all of them sniffle.

"Great," said Sufyaan in disgust, "we don't have a phone either, because Aunty Sophia said we didn't need it! Now what are we going to do? Shouting doesn't work." He kicked the door in frustration, "stupid door, stupid wind, stupid wedding."

Inaayah saw that he was close to tears, and that he was tired and anxious. She put her arms around him and gave him a hug. She was still his big sister and needed to take care of him.

"Don't worry Sufy, we'll soon be off this windy roof, I promise; but we all need to think carefully.

There has to be a way that we can attract the attention of someone."

Inaayah bit her lower lip and concentrated. She had to find a solution, since Uncle Frederick seemed completely hopeless in his misery and Sufyaan was too exhausted to be put his mind to any practical thought.

"I've got it!" she cried, a few moments later, "We came up how many floors?"

"I think there are two or three floors below us and the function is taking place on the second floor," replied Fredrick, looking enquiringly at Inaayah. Her carefully plaited hair was loose and blowing around her face; she was impatiently brushing it back, but her eyes were bright with confidence and determination.

"If you think we can climb down, like they do in the films, I'm afraid it's not going to work, because firstly, I'm scared of heights and secondly, as far as I know, the windows on this building don't have any sills." Frederick said firmly; he obviously didn't trust her ideas.

"No, it's not that," said Inaayah impatiently waving her hands about, "I want to know how many metres down it is to the second floor?"

Sufyaan went to the edge of the roof and peered down, "About twenty or thirty, I guess," he said doubtfully.

"What if we tied something to end of a rope and lowered it down and hit one of the windows to attract attention? The noise would make the people in the room investigate, to find out what was going on."

Fredrick smiled at Inaayah admiringly, "Clever girl, I bet you're the best in class aren't you?"

Inaayah tried to smile modestly, but it was difficult to be modest when it was true, instead, she nodded in agreement and then both she and Frederick burst out laughing at the same time.

Chapter 10

Frederick walked over to where he had been sitting previously and picking up his fancy tall turban, began to unwind the sparkly, gold cloth around it.

"Will this do?" he asked looking across at Inaayah.

"Perfect!" cried Inaayah, "We can tie a shoe or something at the end of it and lower it down. I know that the room, where the kitchen staff were waiting, is directly below us. I'm sure one of them will notice and come up to see what's going on."

Sufyaan said crossly, "What are you two going on about? What rope? what cloth?"

"The turban, silly; and the ruffles on my dress! I can undo them; there must be metres and metres of the horrible stuff, and if we unravel Frederick's turban as well, we can make a rope and tie a shoe at the end of it. Then, if we swing it down and hit a window, Bingo! We're saved!"

Frederick held up what he had unwound, it was only about three metres.

"That's never enough," he commented.

"Just be patient," said Inaayah and she pulled at the seams between the frilly ribbon and the main body of the dress. She held the end of a thread and tugged carefully. As if it by magic, the frills unfurled, layer after layer, like apple peel. A huge sense of satsfaction filled her as she undid the frills, her revenge at the dress that had made her life a misery for the past few months.

"Let me help you," said Fredrick, "I'll unpick those near the bottom of the dress, whilst you do those on the top part."

Sufyaan watched as the two of them pulled away at the frills, unravelling tier after tier of purple ribbon, until there was a coiled heap next to Inaayah.

"Don't just stand there, Sufy," Inaayah called over, "Make yourself useful. Start tying the ends of the ribbon together."

Sufyaan's face broke into a smile as he suddenly understood what Inaayah and Frederick were up to and he set to work.

The three of them worked feverishly and in silence. By the end of what seemed a very long time, but was actually no more than ten minutes, they had a long length of purple rope, which they looped through the piece of golden cloth that had been wrapped around Fredrick's turban.

Inaayah prayed that the plan would work, otherwise how would she be able to justify the destruction of her dress to her parents, Aunty Sophia, Aunt Kanza, and even Mrs Gomez, who had made it with so much care and love? They would be convinced she had done this out of naughtiness and then her life would be practically over, she thought with grim certainty.

"We'll have to use your shoe, Uncle Frederick," said Inaayah, focussing her thoughts into the immediate task."It's the heaviest and the biggest."

"Gosh, they're as long as a boat" Sufyaan examining the fancy slipper shoes that Fredrick had on.

"They're long because they're so narrow; they have a silly curly tip, like a jokey moustache, so my feet actually stop way before the end." Fredrick took them off without a single protest, "Anyway, they're jolly uncomfortable, so I'm only too happy to be rid of them."

"Make sure you make a tight knot" ordered Inaayah, as Fredrick wound the ribbon around the middle of the shoe. She really hoped that the plan would suceed otherwise she would look a fool in front of Frederick and she couldn't bear that.

"I was a boy scout, I'd have you know," he retorted, "I earned a special badge for my knots. Right, let's lower this down, easy now... give me a bit more slack there. OK, now... let's swing it so it hits the window, gently does it. One, two and nope, missed. OK, one more time, yes! Bulls eye! oh, oh, it's getting loose; yikes, I think it's gone! Blow, we've lost the blessed shoe!" Frederick wrapped the ribbon around his hand and snatched it up.

"It's just missed the bloke standing by the entrance of the hotel!" Sufyaan shouted to them as he watched the shoe tumble down, "But he hasn't even looked up to see where it's come from. I bet he's on his phone."

"I think we need some more ribbon and another shoe," said Inaayah. She held out her hands for Frederick to give her his other shoe. Frederick got off from the floor, and brushed the front of his tunic which was now more dusty grey, than golden.

"Good job you've got another to spare," grinned Sufyaan, "you've obviously forgotten your scout skills though."

Inaayah was becoming impatient and worried; she held out her hand for the shoe.

Fredrick didn't reply to Sufyaan, but pointed at his cumber band, "I think I'll take that as well, young man."

Sufyaan looked at Frederick in disbelief, "Are you asking me to take off my cumber band?"

"Indeed I am."

"But, you've got enough length of ribbon, why do you need this? My whole outfit will be spoilt if I take it off!"

Fredrick was unmoved and pointed at Sufyaan's waist again.

"C'mon mate, let's have it, pronto ."

"Come on, Sufyaan, it's important." said Inaayah in annoyance, "Don't waste time, haha," she turned to Fredrick, "Do you get it, waste, waist?" Frederick's blank look told her that he didn't or wouldn't, but it made her feel better anyway.

"Oh well," she shrugged, good naturedly, "never mind, perhaps this isn't the time for puns."

Sufyaan began to slowly and reluctantly unwind the sash from his waist, muttering all the while about 'bossy people'.

Fredrick took the sash from him and knotted it firmly with the existing rope. He then wrapped the ribbon tightly around his other shoe and secured it firmly with a double knot.

Inaayah watched impatiently; why didn't he hurry up? Frederick was one of those people that could not be rushed, she could see that in his deliberate, methodical manner, so different to herself, but it made her agitated to stand back and only watch.

"May I swing it? Please? I promise I will be careful. Oh, please?" she wanted to do something, anything; it was agonising watching Frederick and with her usual self-confidence, she was sure she could do a far better job, especially as she played hockey at school and was very good at applying just the right amount of power to the stick to slip the wooden ball into the net.

Frederick looked at her with his half smile; he looked very nice when he smiled, and his eyes crinkled in a kind sort of way

'He's good man, I'm sure he and Aunt Kanza will be very happy together,' and this thought made Inaayah feel happy.

Inaayah lay flat on her front and swung the shoe in a wide arc and then let it bang against one of the windows. She could see the tops of peoples' heads far below her and she prayed that maybe, just maybe, someone might look up and see them and realise that they were stuck there, 'but more likely they will think we are up to no good and phone the police, which would still be a good thing, although what Mama and Abu will say, I hate to think.'

She concentrated hard, trying to aim the shoe at the window. The shoe hit the window again, and this time, even they could hear the thud it made.

"Let's leave the shoe to dangle for a few minutes, shall we?" suggested Frederick, "so if anyone does hear the banging, they can see the cause of the noise."

Sufyaan was on his stomach next to Inaayah, singing 'What shall we do with a drunken sailor?' at the top of his voice. He was relishing the opportunity to be noisy without being reprimanded and to compensate for the loss of his beloved cumber band.

"Good idea," said Inaayah to Frederick, "I'll tie it to this water drain, whoops! It nearly went there, but it's fine now."

Frederick lay down besides them, their three heads just hanging over the small wall running around the perimeter of the roof space.

"Hope you're not feeling scared, Uncle Frederick?" joked Inaayah.

"I'm surprisingly relaxed, it's very peaceful here, you can hardly hear the traffic down below," he replied, "Mind you, Sufyaan is making enough racket to rival the din of the wretched seagulls."

"I'm trying to help," said Sufyaan indignantly, "Since you two won't let me do anything else, I may as well make some noise."

Frederick laughed, crinkling his eyes again, "No complaints from me, mate. Tell you what, why don't we all sing? It'll past the time at any rate."

So, at Inaayah's suggestion, the three of them sang all the verses of "Drunken sailor' all over again, the whole of, 'My Bonnie lies over the ocean', and they were half way through singing an Irish song called, 'Wild Rover', which Frederick was teaching them, when they heard someone behind them.

"Hello there guys," said a familiar warm voice, "Are you guys alright here? Or are you in the habit of throwing shoes off tall buildings?"

"Jayson!" cried both the children, scrambling to their feet and rushing to give Jayson a hug, "we're so happy to see you!"

"The door shut behind us and…"

"A gust of wind…"

"Uncle Frederick was here and we…"

"…shoe fell and he used my cumber band…"

"Whoa!" Jayson held his hands up in mock alarm, "One at a time, guys, I've only got one pair of ears!"

"How did you know to come upstairs, Jayson?" demanded Inaayah, she had never been more pleased to see anyone before in her whole life.

"I'd seen you two go up the stairs earlier, and when I saw that purple rope dangling in front of the serving room window, it looked familiar; and then I remembered that you were wearing a dress with lots of purple stuff. I also know that this door is liable to close with the wind; it's not the first time that people have got stuck here, that's why there is a notice forbidding anyone coming out to the roof." He shook his finger at them sternly.

"I'm so glad, you're here, Jayson." Sufyaan gave Jayson another hug, "I was worried that Uncle Frederick would have us making a long rope with the rest of our clothes so that we could shimmy down from the roof, like Batman!"

Jayson laughed and then he noticed Frederick standing in his socks, "Good afternoon, Sir," he said politely.

Frederick looked rather embarrassed, he coughed a bit and ran his finger around the tight collar of his tunic,

"Er, Hello, er, Jayson. Thank you for coming upstairs to open the door. Any news from the wedding downstairs? How are things going?" his face was redding as he spoke..

"They are waiting for the groom, Sir," Jayson replied, "May I presume, sir, that you are he?"

Inaayah giggled, Frederick looked embarrassed, but Jayson was very straight faced and polite.

"Presume away," Frederick said, blushing even more, "I suppose I should get down there, although God knows what they are all going to say."

Inaayah said, "Don't worry, Uncle Frederick; we can call you that can't we? Especially now you are going to marry Aunt Kanza. We're right with you. We can be alibis for each other."

Sufyaan went up to him and he and Inaayah each took one of his hands. Inaayah looked at him encouragingly,

"We can say that we got stuck here, together, no one needs to know that you were here ages before us."

"Nope, no body," added Sufyaan with a wink, "That is a secret we will keep for ever and ever, isn't that so Inaayah?"

"Shall we go then?" interrupted Jayson, looking worriedly at the door, "I don't want that door to bang shut again, this time with me stuck here with you. That would be asking for trouble."

Uncle Frederick shrugged himself straight and said firmly, "Right, lead on Jayson. We're right behind you."

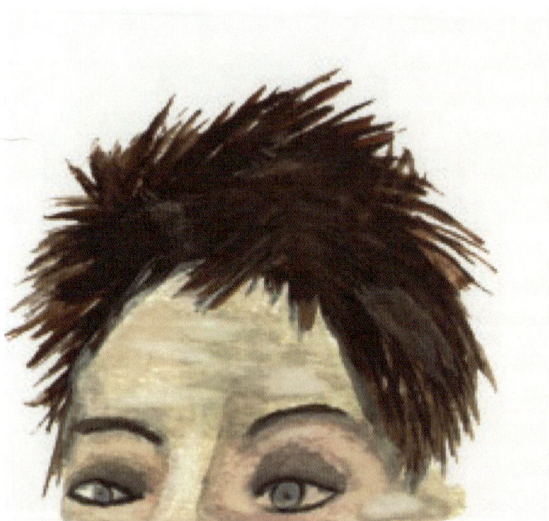

Chapter 11

When they entered the hall, there was an immediate commotion, everyone rushed over to Frederick, fussing and screaming questions at him,

"Where have you been?"

"We've been looking all over for you,"

"Kanza is crying her eyes out, worried sick! She thought you'd had an accident!"

"Darling! Dad and I have been so concerned!"

"The Imam is waiting!"

The children crept away to stand next to the other maids of honour and the pages who were, by this stage, looking exhausted and frustrated.

"What have you done with your dress?" demanded the girl, Mona.

"You aren't half going to be in trouble when Aunt Neena sees what a filthy state it's in, as if you have been rolling on the ground in it."

"What a nasty person she is,'thought Inaayah, "she badly wants me to get into trouble with her precious Aunt Neena.'

Inaayah looked at the girl coolly, with an air of indifference.

 "I did it on purpose; I think it looks far better than before."

In spite of her defiant words though, Inaayah was worried; after all her complaints about the dress, she knew her mother would never believe her explanations. Mona gave her a sneer and turned her back on her.

Inaayah looked across at Sufyaan who was doing his own explaining. The small page boy was demanding to know what Sufyaan had done with his cumber band.

"I used it to save the groom," said Sufyaan, grandly, "He was in danger, see, and I took it off to rescue him from a great height, where he'd got stuck. He didn't know how to get down and it was the only way to bring him to the wedding, so that he can marry Aunt Kanza, like he's meant to.

I'm sure he's probably going to give me a big reward soon, seeing that it was my cumber band that actually got him back here; in fact, I'm sure Aunt Kanza owes me too, 'cos without me she'd never get to marry him."

"Shut it!" hissed the older boy, white with rage, "you and your stupid stories! I'll reward you with a punch, if you don't put a zip in it."

Inaayah was about to intervene, when she heard a loud voice calling her,

"Inaayah! Sufyaan! Come here, please." It was Frederick, he was smiling and relaxed, so different from the worried Frederick of the roof top. He spoke into the microphone so that everyone could hear,

"I'd like to thank Inaayah and Sufyaan for being such good friends and for saving the day, in lots of ways. Without them, I don't think I would be feeling the way I'm feeling now, happy and confident that I am doing the right thing, marrying the love of my life," and here he took Kanza's hand and kissed it, "So, thank you, and I would like you to be my best man, both of you."

Inaayah and Sufyaan grinned with joy. Inaayah noted with satisfaction the look of amazement in her parent's eyes as they wondered what on earth the two of them had been up to, the look of resentment in Mona's narrowed eyes and the puzzled expressions of Aunty Sophia and Mrs Gomez as they realised that Inaayah's dress was very, very different to the one she had been wearing earlier.

It was turning into a better wedding than she had ever hoped for.

Aunt Kanza's voice broke into her happy thoughts, "Frederick, where on earth are your shoes?"

Frederick, Inaayah and Sufyaan all looked at one another and burst out laughing.

20402404R00050

Printed in Great Britain
by Amazon